Rowan Skysong and the Starfinders

Rowan Skysong and the Starfinders

Michelle Mohrweis

Illustrated by

Fran Cesarano

Collins

Chapter 1

I'm not nervous.

I'm not! I shouldn't get nervous, not when I've planned *everything* perfectly and have been practising for weeks. Sure, my hands are shaking, and my stomach feels like it's tied into a knot bigger than Earth itself, but I'm not nervous.

OK. Maybe I'm a little nervous.

I can't help it though! This is the biggest day of my life. Today's test will change everything.

"Come on, Rowan," I mutter to myself as I float upside down, staring at the metal walls of my bedroom. "You're fine. You've got to be fine. It's time to focus and not be a scaredy cat."

My walls are painted with constellations, specks of yellow and white scattered between the cabinets, handholds and warm lights. Mama helped me paint them to match the star charts painted all around the hallways of our starship.

We're Starfinders, so naturally we love stars.

Right now, staring at the walls does help me feel a little calmer. Still, I can't help biting on my necklace – a star-shaped one Mum got me when we visited Pluto last month – to try and calm down more.

It's just so hard to *not* be nervous, when my mothers are the most famous Starfinders ever. Everyone expects me to be amazing too. Which means I 1,000% can't fail today's test.

A small sound chimes from my side. I look at my holopad, which is clipped to my flight suit trousers so it won't float away in the low gravity.

There are 14 minutes until the big test.

I can do this. I can handle it. I've got a plan: a really good, secret plan.

With one last bite on my necklace, I push off my bedroom wall and float towards the door. Outside is the Starfinder Apprentice common room.

"X-ray sensors can monitor solar activity. UV sensors can detect ultraviolet radiation – " Varl, my best friend, floats past me, muttering under his breath. Varl's from a planet in the Andromeda galaxy, where everyone has feathery hair and bright freckles that sometimes glow. Right now, his feathers are all puffed up, which means he's nervous too.

Varl's one of the smartest people I know and will hopefully be my partner for the test. If he's nervous …

That Earth-sized knot in my stomach swells into a Saturn-sized tangle.

"You two are ridiculous," Lizel, another apprentice, states as she floats by. "Neither of you should be scared."

Lizel is from the Milky Way galaxy, just like me. Only her solar system is on the opposite side of the galaxy from Earth's and everyone on her home planet has four arms and breathes nitrogen instead of oxygen.

"I – " Words fail me.

Lizel rolls her eyes. "What was the first galaxy the early Starfinders visited outside their own 300 years ago?"

"The Milky Way," I say immediately.

There's a reason a lot of humans (like me and Mum!) are Starfinders. Earth was the first planet the original Starfinders visited, and since the ancient humans already loved to explore space, they joined the Starfinders right away.

"Right. And what do Starfinders do?"

"We map the stars, search for distant planets, and help everywhere we can. We'll never stop until we've reached the edge of the universe!" The familiar words are more calming than anything else.

"Yes!" Lizel grins under her clear breathing mask. She's the bravest person I know, and *never* gets scared. "See? You're ready. No reason to be nervous. We've been preparing for this *forever.*"

"Technically, it's been two years, three days and one hour," comments Varl. He grabs a handrail to slow himself down and float next to us.

"Like I said, *forever.*"

"We're all ready for this," I repeat, even though my stomach is still a little twisty. I look at the big viewport that takes up an entire wall of the common room. "Ready to explore *out there*."

Outside, a planet with swirling white and emerald clouds comes into view as our starship turns. I sigh, floating closer until my nose bumps against the chilly glass.

Pressed this close to the viewport, it's like space is everywhere around me.

There's the planet below, with small silvery spacecraft flying in and out of its clouds. In the distance, three bright spots glow where the planet's moons are, and beyond those are countless stars twinkling in the endless expanse of space.

We're almost two million light years away from Earth – where Mum grew up and where I was born – floating through space in the biggest Starfinder spacecraft ever.

This is what it's all about.

I want to be out there. I want to map those stars and visit distant worlds, to discover someplace nobody from our galaxy has ever been before. I want to be like my mums.

I want to be a Starfinder.

But before I can be one, I *have* to pass today's Apprentice Test.

"Are you ready for, you know?" whispers Varl.

I nod. Varl's been helping me nonstop with my secret plan. He doesn't care about being famous – he just wants to pass the test – but he's super good with reading data and maths, so I convinced him to help me last year.

"I'm just so nervous," Varl keeps whispering. "This is going to be so cool, but what if we don't have the right sensors? What if we miss our chance to get the data? What if – ”

“Has anyone seen my cloak?” Jazz Rodrigo, another apprentice, tumbles into the common room, interrupting Varl’s spiral.

Reluctantly, I pull away from the viewport to look around. A bit of blue cloth covered in stars – silver stars since we’re still apprentices – is stuck to the air vent in the corner.

"Over there," I say, fidgeting with my own mini shoulder cloak.

"Oh, thank goodness!" Jazz pushes off from the holotable, and floats over to grab it. "I can't believe I almost lost it!"

I try to not roll my eyes. Jazz is always getting distracted and losing stuff. She never seems to care about science or data, is late to half our classes, and is always reading books and asking about stories instead. I don't understand her at all.

She's the last person I'd *ever* want to work with on the test.

Tiiiiiiiiiiiing

A gentle chiming sounds from my holopad. I glance at the screen. Ten minutes until the test.

"Come on," I say, pushing off a handrail to float towards the door. "We can't be late!"

Varl, Lizel, Jazz and a few other apprentices follow. It's time to take the Apprentice Test. Time to determine our futures.

Chapter 2

As I float towards the cargo bay, where the Apprentice Test will start, my nerves swell from that Saturn-sized tangle into a sun-sized monster.

Mum and Mama wait inside, near a stage with all our other teachers.

I gulp. This is it.

I activate my own grav shoes, bracing myself as the magnets pull me down to the floor with a *thud.*

"Are you ready?" Mum asks, when I clomp over.

"Of course I am!" I say, shoving all my nerves deep, deep down. "I'm going to make you super proud."

"You already make me proud," Mum laughs, as she nudges my shoulder.

"You'll do wonderfully," adds Mama from beside her.

I pretend to smile, even as Mama peels away to start the Apprentice Test ceremony.

Mum and Mama might say that, but I know it won't be enough if I fail. My mums are *amazing*! Mum's the leader of the Starfinders, and Mama is the best Starfinder teacher in years. Ever since Mum and Mama met,

when I was three years old, they've done tons of amazing stuff, like helping planets form peace treaties, getting more people to join the Starfinders, and making new science discoveries! I *have* to do well, to show my mothers that I'm worth being proud of. To show the world I'm as good as them.

Which is why I have my secret plan.

"Welcome, young apprentices!" Mama announces, in her song-like voice that always grabs people's attention. "Today marks the start of a new journey, a new opportunity. Today you will partner with another apprentice and fly out to the anomaly to demonstrate your skills as a Starfinder."

"This is so exciting!" whispers Lizel.

"And nerve-wracking!" adds Varl.

"I can't wait to see the anomaly," sighs Jazz.

The anomaly appears once every year. Nobody really knows what it is, but it messes with the space around it and only lasts for a few minutes every year. Mum says that measuring it has been part of the Apprentice Test since before she was even born.

"As Starfinders, we seek to learn and share knowledge, to map the stars and help the galaxies however we can. Remember, we'll always keep exploring until we find the end of the universe."

Mama pauses to grin at the famous Starfinder saying. The universe is always expanding, which means it's impossible to find the end of it. That's our way of saying that Starfinders will *never* stop exploring.

"Teamwork and cooperation are important parts of being a Starfinder," continues Mama, after a moment. "Thus, your teachers have paired you with another apprentice. Look at your pairings and begin your test."

Beside me, Varl whispers to himself like a chant, "Please be Rowan. Please be Rowan."

Nearby, our teachers type something into their holopads. A second later, our own holopads vibrate.

Please be Varl. Please be Varl, I think in an echo

of my friend's whisper. *It has to be Varl.* Varl's helped me a ton with my plan and works with me on every project. Our teachers know we work best together. They'll have to pair us together, right? Only, when I look at the holopad, my heart sinks. I'm not partnered with Varl.

I'm partnered with Jazz Rodrigo.

Chapter 3

Here's the thing about Jazz: I don't dislike her. I just don't understand her.

I'm autistic and ADHD, like Mum. My world has to be in order; I need to know where things are, so I don't lose them. I need to have a schedule and routine, or I get stressed. I like to look at everything logically, to piece clues together until I have the information I need, like when digging through satellite data and spacecraft logs.

You'd think Jazz would be the same. She's autistic and ADHD too. I know because I've heard her tell people that in class before.

Except, she's not the same.

Jazz is chaos; always rushing to class late, always spacing out and forgetting stuff. Jazz likes to derail a perfectly good science class by asking a bajillion questions about stories from whatever planet we're studying instead. Jazz is … confusing.

Right now, when I'm determined to pull off my secret plan and be the best Starfinder ever, just the thought of that chaos *really* stresses me out.

But here I am: working with Jazz Rodrigo.

We're about to leave for the test using the Apprentice 3 – a small research spacecraft that apprentices are trained in. It's just big enough for me and Jazz, with a cockpit, a small galley with food stored in the cabinets and a holotable in the middle, and two closet-sized rooms. We won't be gone long enough to need more.

If Varl was here, it would be perfect. Without my best friend beside me though …

"Come on, Jazz," I snap. She's floating near the ceiling of our spacecraft, staring at the stars that are painted onto it and spacing out again. "Jazz. Jaaaaaazzzz."

Varl never spaces out. If Varl was my partner, we'd already be hunched over the pilot controls, figuring out how to pull off my plan.

"Jazz!"

She looks startled, then laughs a little, like this isn't the most stressful day ever. "Sorry! Got lost in thought. What's up?"

"You need to buckle in."

"Oh! Are we clear for launch already?" Jazz pulls herself down to the cockpit chairs and straps in. "Want me to fly?"

"I've got it."

"Are you sure? 'Cause I'm really good at piloting these."

"I said I've got it," I insist.

Jazz frowns at me.

I ignore her, starting up the pre-flight checks

instead. If Varl was here with me, he'd be flying while I made sure all our ship's sensors were working.

Instead, I'm with Jazz, and I'm not gonna let her mess this up.

The Apprentice 3 whirs to life as I flip a few switches and tap at the control screen. The lever and yoke, which let me control where the ship goes, pop out of the control panel. I cling tight to the yoke with one hand and the lever with the other, making sure to clear the inner doors as I inch us forward into the nearest airlock.

THUMP.

"Oh look, you hit the floor," comments Jazz, dryly.

"I brushed it. Lightly," I growl through gritted teeth. I nudge the yoke to the left.

SCRAAAAPE.

"And you scraped the door." Jazz flips through her holopad screens. "Flight control says nothing damaged, but to be more careful. Are you sure you don't want me to fly?"

"No. I've got this."

It takes way too long for me to inch us the rest of the way into the airlock, then fly out into space towards the anomaly's coordinates. The entire way, Jazz won't stop making little comments about my flying.

"I didn't – oof – know it was – ugh – possible for spaceflight to be *this* bumpy," complains Jazz.

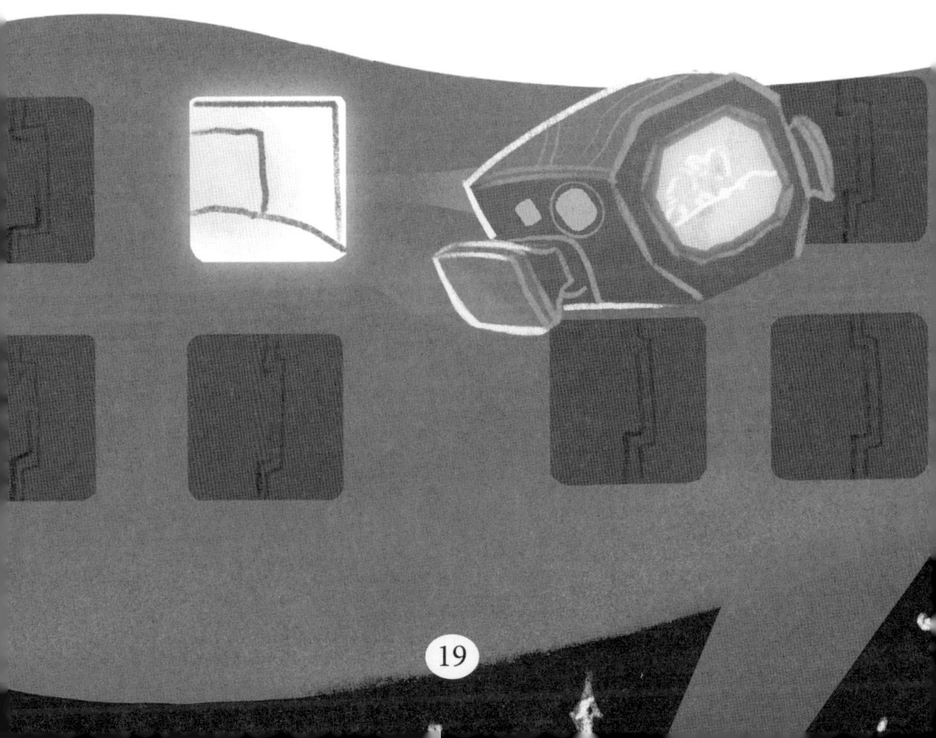

I grit my teeth harder. Everything about today is going wrong, but I refuse to let it get worse. I'm going to pass the test. I'm going to pull off my secret plan, even if I don't have Varl to help me. I'm going to be the most famous Starfinder ever.

Eventually, we reach the test coordinates, and I slow the spacecraft down with the reverse thrusters.

"OK," I say. "The anomaly will appear any minute now. Let's get ready to get the readings."

"Can we park further back?" asks Jazz. "We'll get better pictures further away."

"I want some wavelength readings. Those will be better closer."

"Well, I'd rather we take pictures. Either way works for the test, and pictures are more fun." Jazz frowns at me as she talks.

I scowl back. "Too bad. I'm the one flying. I say we park close enough for wavelength data."

Here's the thing. Normally I wouldn't care what type of data we get on the anomaly.

Wavelength readings, pictures and so on. I love it all. Except, I *need* a specific type for my plan.

It's not enough to just take measurements and pass the test. I want to do something bigger; I want to find a whole new galaxy.

Varl and I came up with the plan last year.

I was bored one day and digging through old satellite data when I noticed it. During the anomaly, the closest satellites started detecting a gas giant orbiting a G-type star. That isn't anything too weird. G-type stars are super common, and gas giants usually form around them. Earth's star is a G-type, and we have *four* gas giants in our solar system: Jupiter, Saturn, Uranus and Neptune.

Only, there aren't as many gas giants in the section of space we're hanging out near now, and I couldn't find a single star chart showing a G-type star with a gas giant in the direction the satellites were pointing.

Which means it might be an unknown one.

During the anomaly, stuff gets weird sometimes.

Like, time slows down a little. Space stretches out near it. Some Starfinders even claim that the satellite sensors start working better, seeing further.

I'm pretty sure that the satellite saw a gas giant in a galaxy no Starfinder has ever been to yet. The wavelength readings will let me prove it for sure.

I'll be the first apprentice who ever discovered a new galaxy! Or, new to us, anyway, since other people might already live there.

I should probably explain some of this to Jazz, at least enough to get her off my back. Only, before I say anything, Jazz rolls her eyes, unbuckles herself, and lunges for the ship's controls.

"Hey!" I shout. "What gives?"

"We're going to take pictures," Jazz says, yanking our little ship around as she floats half in front of me. "Which means we need more distance."

"Well, I want," I grab the controls back as I talk, pushing Jazz out of the way, "to get wavelength data, which means we need to be closer!" Our ship lurches forward a few yards.

"Too bad. We're getting pictures. You flew the ship, so I get to decide the data we collect!" The ship spins back around.

"That's not how it works!" I shout.

"That's how it's working now. I'm not gonna fail the test just because you won't let me do *anything*." Jazz glares at me, clinging to the controls just above where I'm grabbing them.

"If you fail, it's not my fault! We're staying here." I glare back and pull hard on the controls. The ship shudders, then jolts to the side.

"Urg!" yells Jazz, grabbing the controls and yanking the ship back a metre. "This is supposed to be teamwork! You're not letting me help!"

"I – "

Suddenly, the ship lurches forward *again*. Only this time, it's way too fast and neither of us caused it.

Jazz shrieks as she's sent flying towards the viewscreen. I reach out and grab her just in time as the ship shakes.

"What's happening?" she screams.

"I don't know!"

I pull Jazz back towards me until she can grab onto her seat and buckle in, then lean around to stare out of the window. Outside, where empty space was before, the air is lit with purple and blue lightning. Strange globs of energy float between the lightning, drifting all around us.

It's …

It's …

"It's the anomaly," gasps Jazz. "We're too close!"

The ship lurches forward again. The anomaly is pulling us in!

I grab the controls, trying to fly further away. For a second, it's working. We pull out of the globs of colourful light, back towards open space. Then …

CRACK.

A bolt of purple lightning hits the spacecraft.

All my controls go dead.

"Oh no," I whisper.

"Yikes," squeaks Jazz.

Then our ship jolts forward once more and there's no time to do anything but cling to our seats. With a lurch, then another, then a *massive* jolt, we tumble into the centre of the anomaly.

Chapter 4

It feels like the ship is tumbling and spinning for *ages.*

Jazz and I cling to our seats and scream. All around us the air is blurry. We're moving so fast, too fast!

Stuff falls from the cabinets. The force of our spinning and tumbling makes the stuff fly all around the ship. A wrench crashes into the viewport. A hairbrush slams into the control panel. A food pouch smacks into my face.

Then suddenly the ship jolts again … and everything stops.

I groan, feeling queasy. I push the food

pouch away, then watch as it floats towards Jazz. She stares back at me with wide eyes.

"Is ... is it over?" she asks cautiously. We're not spinning around anymore. We're not really moving at all.

Together, we look towards the viewscreen.

Outside, there are no globs of energy. No crackling lightning. Just peaceful space with stars twinkling in the distance.

"I think so," I whisper. "What happened?"

Jazz leans forward and presses the communication button on the control panel. "Apprentice 3 to Starfinder Home. We need help."

Nobody answers.

Jazz frowns, flipping a switch. "Weird. This says that our communication system should still be working." She presses the button again, opening a line to the starship. "Apprentice 3 to Starfinder Home. Do you hear us?"

There's no reply.

I reach over and flip the emergency reboot switch. After a second, the engines whir to life and the screens flicker back on. The yoke and levers light up, showing that they're working again. Carefully, I turn the Apprentice 3 in a big circle.

"Where's the starship?" whispers Jazz. "Where's the planet?"

Around us is nothing but empty space. No planet with swirling clouds and three moons. No Starfinder Starship, or any spacecraft at all.

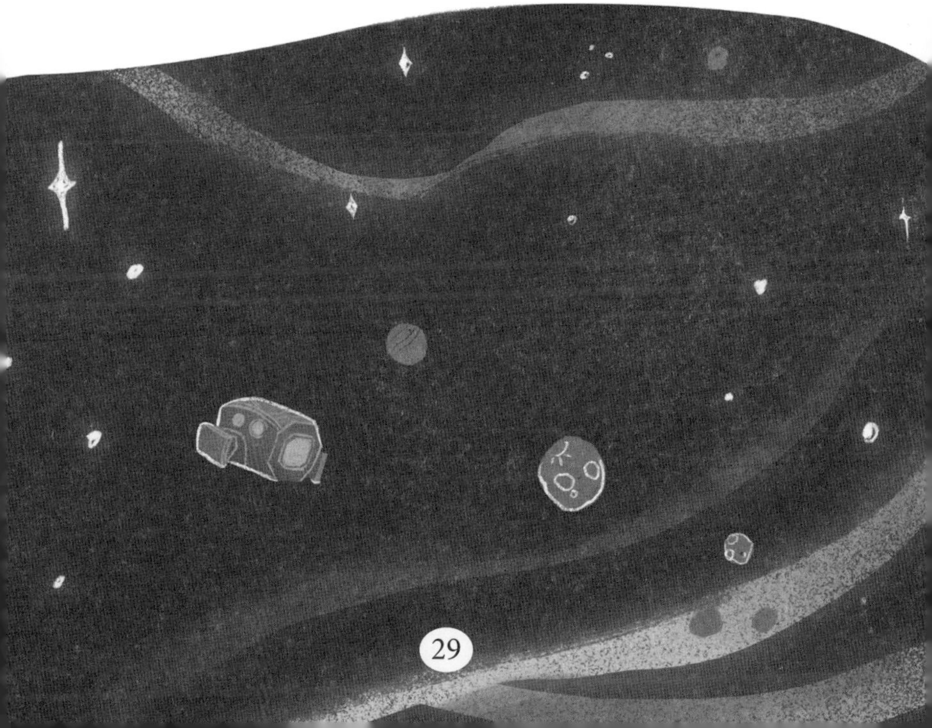

Then I turn us a little further and gasp.

There *is* something here, but it's not the planet or starship. There's an asteroid field floating behind us, massive asteroids and smaller rocks drifting all over, with pink, purple and blue dust sparkling between it. It stretches out like a piece of ribbon, disappearing somewhere off into distant space.

I've seen asteroid fields before, but never any that look so colourful and *never* any with the asteroids so close together.

"Where *are* we?" I ask.

"I don't know," Jazz gasps. She unbuckles her seat and pushes herself through the air to the holotable. "I'll get a scan of outside."

I follow, activating my grav boots and thunking down onto the spacecraft floor to avoid drifting past the table. "I'll run it through the Star Map Collection."

Only, I have a sinking feeling in my stomach. A feeling that makes dread collect like the dust between the asteroids.

Still, I set to work. The holotable whirs as I plug in Jazz's readings, telling the program to compare them to its star charts. It'll match the sky we see outside to one of the known star charts, and then we can figure out where we are.

For a minute, the program loads star chart after star chart. Then it blinks a message back at us. A really, really bad message.

Location Not Found

I run the program again.

Location Not Found

I load up a different program, one that basically does the same thing, but was made by some scientists over in the Triangulum Galaxy instead.

Location Not Found

"Rowan," whispers Jazz. She hugs her hands around herself and disengages her grav boots, floating up into the air. "I don't think we're in the Milky Way galaxy anymore."

"That's not possible," I insist. I run the

program again.

Location Not Found

"No no no no!" I run it again. Then again.

Starfinders have been exploring the galaxies for centuries. It doesn't matter that stars look different depending on where you are. It doesn't matter if every planet sees different constellations. We have star charts for them all.

Except, no matter how many times I run the program, the message is always the same.

Location Not Found

Chapter 5

Jazz and I spend the next hour trying everything we can think of.

We run every program that we have to compare star charts. We send out multiple messages from the ship's communication system. I take some readings of the nearest star (a G-type star like the Earth's sun, but way bigger), then start looking for any data in the holotable on stars with similar readings.

Nothing. Nobody has ever logged this star.

There are a few planets we detect. A small, rocky planet somewhere on the other side of the asteroid field. Two Earth-sized planets somewhere a few million kilometres away. A gas giant that's only a day away from our location. That one gives me a really, really bad feeling. We can't be in my mystery galaxy. We can't! Because if we are, that means we're really, really, really far away from home.

All at once, it's way too overwhelming. I push myself away from the holotable and towards one of the bedrooms, yanking the thick fabric door closed.

The bedroom is small, the size of a closet. It has a sleeping bag on the wall that I can zip myself into, so I don't float into anything important while sleeping and a set of drawers for personal stuff. The drawers are empty right now. I didn't bring any of my stuff since the test wasn't supposed to take long.

I sniffle, then hit the wall with my hand. I hit it again, then again, like that can force all my feelings out of myself and into the soft padded fabric of the little bedroom. Again and again and again. I can't stop, I can't help it.

Everything is *too much.*

Too much noise from the Apprentice 3's engines.

Too much light searing into my eyes.

Too many horrible thoughts spin spin spinning in my head.

I know how to read star charts. I know how to understand our spacecraft's sensor data. I'm good at piecing clues together. Right now, the clues say we're stuck really, really far from home.

I start crying, big sobs that come with a gross stuffy nose and tears that gather around my eyes, clinging to my skin. The soft walls absorb my hits, and I cry and cry and cry.

Eventually, the feeling of everything being *too much* fades just enough that I realise I'm having a meltdown.

I press a switch next to the sleeping bag, then sniffle as the lights dim and the bedroom's sound dampeners kick on, muffling the noises outside. With everything softer and quieter, a little more of everything that's *too much* fades away.

As the *too much* fades, I get tired instead. It's that post meltdown tired, where my bones feel heavy even in the low gravity, and everything feels too sharp, but at least I'm myself again.

My tears slow enough that I can wipe them away and stare out of the tiny viewport.

Outside, dust from the asteroid field blurs together into a ribbon of pinks and blues and purples. It reminds me of the flag Mum has hanging in our living quarters on the starship, the one I lived in before I moved to the apprentice dorms.

There are so many pretty stars outside the

window too. At least some of those have to be the same stars we see from home, right?

This wasn't supposed to happen. I was supposed to get proof the mystery galaxy existed, not get thrown who knows how many light years across space to end up in it. Not completely lost in an unknown part of space.

Still, there has to be a way to find where we are.

A way to get back home.

Chapter 6

When I finally leave my room, Jazz is floating upside down over the holotable, her dark hair brushing the screen. She's reading a massive book.

"Hi," she says. "I think I know what happened, if you want to hear."

I do. "So, what happened then?"

Jazz takes a shaky breath, then flips the book so I can see. There's a picture drawn in it, showing a field of colourful grass.

"I got this book of legends on Hyverni, the planet we were orbiting," she says, fidgeting with the top of the pages. "They don't have a lot of books since they mostly tell stories through songs,

so I was really excited when I found it – ”

“And?” I don’t mean to be impatient, but I’m so tired.

“Well, there’s a famous legend from Hyverni.” Jazz lets the book float in front of her and fidgets with her sound dampeners instead. “Supposedly, there was an explorer long ago who sailed into the ocean of stars. Only, he strayed too close to the field of colours, and it ate him.”

"The field of colours? What's that?" I bite my necklace.

"The legend is probably referring to the anomaly and its colours, but it's a legend so it's not super clear. Still, it says that a year later, when the field grew again, two more people followed to find the lost explorer. The field ate them too. After that, they learnt to never venture too close."

I frown at the book's picture. If I squint, the colours on the grass do look kind of like lightning and bubbles, like somebody drew a picture of the anomaly who'd never really seen it, so a lot of the details were wrong.

"So, you think they got too close to the anomaly and got sucked in?"

Jazz nods.

"It's only a legend, but it would explain what happened to us. Usually, nobody gets that close to the anomaly." Jazz winces. "If the original explorers ended up here, like us, and were never seen by anyone on Hyverni again – "

"They might have never found a way home."

"We should have stayed further away," mutters Jazz.

I whip around to glare at her. "*You* shouldn't have tried to take over the controls! We were far enough away at first!"

"I'm sorry, but *you* weren't being a good team-mate!"

"So what? *You* distracted me, and because *you* tried to take over, we ended up getting too close and didn't realise until it was too late!"

"You're so … so … ugh!" yells Jazz. She throws her hands into the air, then yelps as she accidentally hits her book. It spirals uselessly towards the ceiling.

"I'm what?" I demand. "What were you going to say? Huh? Because you're … you're – "

Just then, a small chiming sound comes from the control panel. We both freeze. It comes again.

Tiiiiiing.

"Is that – ?" Jazz gasps.

I float over to the control panel and stare at the screens. The chime sounds again, a small light flashing on one of our display screens.

Tiiiing.

It's our communications channel.

Only, it's not picking up anything from home, or anything we'd expect.

"That's a distress call," I say. "Somebody needs help."

Chapter 7

The distress signal completely distracts us from our argument, and after that it's hard to stay angry. The thing is, we're Starfinders.

Helping people is the most important thing a Starfinder can do, and we're reminded of that in every one of our classes. Which means, even though we're still only apprentices, we need to help whoever's in trouble.

"It's really close," says Jazz, poking at the screen. "We could be there in an hour."

"OK." I hesitate, then glance at Jazz. "Do you want to fly?"

See? I *can* be a good team-mate, no matter what Jazz says.

"Yes!" Jazz pushes herself to the cockpit and settles into the pilot chair.

Soon we're on our way, skirting around the outside of the asteroid field.

The signal grows stronger as we fly. Soon, the source of it comes into view: there's a spacecraft floating near the edge of the asteroid field. Its engines look damaged and there's no power running through them. There are lights in the viewports though.

I frown and lean forward. "I've never seen that type of spacecraft before."

"We should be close enough to call them." Jazz presses the communication button. "Hello! Is anyone there? We got your distress signal."

A second later, the speakers crackle to life and somebody replies. "Oh, thank the stars! Yes! Hello! Please, my name is Alenia of Cloud 3, and I need your help!"

Alenia doesn't tell us anything more until we dock with the spacecraft, even though Jazz asks a million questions over the comms. Like, what went wrong? Why was the ship they're on damaged? What happened? No matter how much Jazz asks, Alenia just states that they'll explain when they see us.

Soon enough we pull up alongside the bigger spacecraft and carefully ease ourselves up to an airlock. They have a different docking mechanism than us, but luckily Starfinders are ready for that. Since we're always exploring and meeting new people, we often find spacecraft that we can't dock with.

Instead of trying to dock, Jazz activates the emergency tunnel. A small plasticky-looking tunnel piece extends out and suctions itself around the other spacecraft's airlock door. Then air hisses as the tunnel pressurises.

"You're safe to come through," says Jazz into the comms.

A minute later, the other ship's outer airlock door opens. Someone with dark brown skin and long black hair looks out. Alenia cautiously floats over to our ship, then peeks inside the airlock. The minute Alenia sees us, their face breaks into a huge smile.

"I knew it!" Alenia laughs, as they float inside our little spacecraft. "You're not from around here, are you?"

"How'd you know?" I ask.

"Your spacecraft is like none I've ever seen," explains Alenia, peering around with wide eyes, "but more importantly, I knew because of your translator devices. They're really good, but they sound

different than ours. They're clearer but have a longer delay."

Jazz floats over. "I'm Jazz Rodrigo. She/her." She sticks out a hand to shake.

Alenia stares at it, in confusion.

Jazz quickly explains. "I have my hand out because where we're from, people hold each other's hands and shake them up and down as a way of greeting each other sometimes. And yeah, we aren't from this solar system … or galaxy."

"Or any galaxy around it," I add glumly.

Alenia grabs Jazz's hand and vigorously shakes it. Then she folds her hand into a fist and makes a complex circle-like motion in the air. "This is how we greet people in this solar system," she explains. "If you do the same thing and match me, it's a way of saying hello."

Jazz mimics the motion.

"I'm Rowan Skysong," I offer, mimicking the motion alongside Jazz. "They/them."

"I am Alenia of Cloud 3. Today I use she/her."

"What happened to your ship?" I peer back through the view screen at the transport ship and its damaged engines. "Is there anyone else on board who needs help, or just you?"

"The others were rescued earlier," explains Alenia. She scowls. "And … well – " Alenia fidgets with one of her braids and bites her lip.

She glances from me to Jazz.

Oh. She's scared.

Something bad must have happened, and she doesn't know if she can trust us. I bite my necklace, twisting the squishy pendant between my teeth. How can I convince Alenia that we want to help? That we're safe?

Luckily, Jazz comes to the rescue. "I know you don't have any reason to trust us," Jazz says calmly. "But we want to help. We're Starfinders. In our galaxies, we travel around mapping the stars, meeting people and helping people. So, if you want to tell us what's going on, we'd like to help. Or, if you don't want to tell us, can you point us to a place where you'll be safe so we can take you there?"

I didn't realise that Jazz was so good at talking to people. It reminds me of Mama, who can make you feel better with just her words.

Alenia blinks at Jazz. Then she straightens her shoulders and nods.

“Very well. I shall tell you.” She takes a deep breath. “The ship was sabotaged … by people who are trying to catch *me*.”

Chapter 8

Over the next half hour, Alenia quietly explains what happened. She's always liked to mess with technology and invent things. Recently, she figured out how to make a gravity device. It can create artificial gravity inside any spaceship, no matter how small. It ended up working really well, so well that CloudsCorp – a massive company that can be found all over this solar system – wanted it.

Alenia refused to sell them her plans, though.

"CloudsCorp will build it, but then make it so expensive that only the richest people can afford it," she snaps. "My device can help so many more people."

Alenia clenches her hands around a set of

blueprints she pulled out of her bag, then quickly loosens her grip to smooth them out again. I don't understand them, but they look really impressive. If the invention works like Alenia claims, that's a big deal.

Many species have a hard time in space, including humans like me and Jazz. Without gravity, our muscles start to deteriorate and our eyesight gets worse. Even bones get weak if we stay in space too long! Usually, we solve that problem by stopping on planets with gravity, to recover, but it would be incredible if we didn't have to.

"So, what happened?" asks Jazz, drawing me back to Alenia and her story. Jazz is back in the pilot seat of the spacecraft, though she hasn't started flying us away yet.

"I told CloudsCorp no. I refused to sell the plans to them. Instead, I'm going to present them to the Council of Planets." Alenia looks super proud as she says that.

"The Council of Planets?" I ask.

"The council runs everything in this solar system," explains Alenia. "If I can convince them that my invention does what I claim, then they'll make sure the plans for it are given to all the engineers throughout all the planets. Then it can help everyone."

"And CloudsCorp didn't want that?" asks Jazz.

"No. They can't sell it and make money if it's something everyone knows how to build." She sighs, picking at a fingernail. "CloudsCorp does stuff like this all the time."

"That's terrible," says Jazz.

"I know!" Alenia scowls. "There are a few people who work for CloudsCorp that aren't so terrible, and they're trying to change things, but right now the people in charge don't care!"

"What happened when you refused to sell the plans?" I ask.

"They tried to stop me from leaving Cloud 3," explains Alenia, "but I was able to get a ticket for a transport ship, and my family helped me sneak out. I thought I was safe until the ship's engines failed. CloudsCorp must have known I'd have to leave on that ship and sabotaged it. One of the people I know who works for the company sent me a message warning me that it was a trap, and that CloudsCorp was going to have people on the rescue ship waiting to try and steal my plans!"

"So, you hid?" asks Jazz.

Alenia nods. "Yes, I hid when the rescue ship showed up and waited until it was gone to reactivate the distress signal. Only, once they realise that I'm not with the others they rescued, they're going to send more ships to look for me."

I shiver, then glance at the control panels, running a quick check.

"Can we take you to the council?" asks Jazz. "If we can find it. We're kind of lost."

Jazz then starts to explain what happened to us. I tune her out though, staring at the control panel screen. Our spacecraft is small, but it's a Starfinder ship, so it has really good sensors. Right now, those sensors are picking something up, but I'm not sure what.

"... so here we are. Lost," Jazz says, off to the side.

"Maybe I can help!" exclaims Alenia. "The council always offers a favour to anyone that presents them with an invention that will help people. If they like my invention, then we can ask for passes to the Sunset Library."

"The Sunset Library?" I ask.

"It's the biggest library in the solar system, but you need the council's permission to visit. It's got so many books! It even has books from before the Great Disaster 100 years ago. That was when a solar flare destroyed most of the technology our solar system relied on. In the panic afterwards a lot of the libraries on our planets got destroyed." She shakes her head sadly, then brightens up again a moment later. "I bet they'll have star charts you can look at from the time when people explored more, before the Great Disaster."

"Sounds like you want to visit, too," laughs Jazz.

"Of course I do! My parents have a library back on Cloud 3, where I'm from, but it's nothing like the Sunset Library. I want to read all the engineering books I can!"

"Hey," I mutter, flipping to a new sensor. "Jazz ... turn off the engines."

"Hold on a sec." She turns away from me, back to Alenia. "Do you know how to get to the council planet from here?"

Alenia pulls out a bulky holopad and types something in. "These are directions to the Planet of Many Sunsets. That's where I was supposed to present my invention to the council."

"Jazz, Alenia," I hiss. "Seriously, we need to hide!"

Outside the viewport, space is cluttered with rock fragments and dust, with the edge of the broken ship just barely in view, clogging everything up. The ship's sensors, though? They're like my extra eyes and the story they tell is *not good.*

"Hide from what?" Jazz asks.

"From that!"

Outside the viewport, space ripples. A second later, a massive spacecraft pops into view. The other ship is at least twice the size as ours, with a claw-like device on the front. It's all shiny silver metal and sharp edges, with the word CloudsCorp painted on one side.

"Oh," whimpers Jazz.

It's too late. Whoever's piloting the other spacecraft has spotted us. They fire up their engines and spin to face us. Then the massive claw on the front is flying our way!

Chapter 9

Jazz yelps and hits a button, releasing the airlock tunnel. Then she yanks the controls to the right, spinning our spacecraft out of the way.

The claw snaps closed right where we had been.

"I told you we needed to hide!" I shout.

"Well, sorry if I didn't believe you! It's not like you ever explain yourself!" Jazz pulls the controls to the left again. We dive away just as the claw shoots back out to try and grab us again.

"Can we please argue less and focus on escaping?" yelps Alenia.

"Working on it!" cries Jazz. She hits the engine

and sends us racing towards the asteroid field. I grit my teeth and grip the edges of my chair, fighting back all the things I want to yell.

Alenia's right. We've got to escape first.

Jazz flips us left, then swings us around an asteroid and presses the acceleration hard. Our ship races ahead and she narrowly slides between two more asteroids, dodging another grab from the claw.

Then she throws our ship to the left, sliding

up and over another asteroid. The CloudsCorp ship can't follow fast enough. It lurches the other way to avoid the asteroid.

"Let's lose them!" Jazz shouts gleefully.

Then she pulls off the most amazing flying I've *ever* seen.

She weaves us between asteroids and over others. She threads us through the smallest gaps and tucks us into the narrowest canyons. She even darts into a tunnel on a really, really big asteroid, then flips the Apprentice 3 around to fly underneath the asteroid when we pop out of the other side. Jazz flies the ship like nothing I've ever seen before!

Soon, we've left the other ship in the dust.

Jazz slows the Apprentice 3, sets us down on top of a medium-sized asteroid, then powers down the engine to make us harder to find.

"I think that did it," she says, peering out of the viewscreen.

I check the sensors, looking for the readings that

warned me about the CloudsCorp ship earlier. They're still picking it up, but it's further away now.

"That worked," I say, relieved. I take a deep breath, then add, "I'm sorry."

Jazz blinks at me. "Huh?"

"I should've explained *why* I wanted you to cut the engines," I rush to say. "I hate it when people don't explain stuff to me, and it's not fair that I did that to you. Also, I shouldn't have been so mean earlier, and I should've let you help from the beginning instead of trying to do everything myself." I stare at my lap as I apologise, fidgeting with my holopad.

"Oh," Jazz shrugs. "That was kinda frustrating. I guess I could have asked why you wanted me to hide instead of ignoring you, though. So, I'm also sorry."

I grin at her, hesitantly. "Maybe

we can both try to be better and work together?"

"Deal. We work together and let each other help!"

We shake on it while Alenia watches, looking kind of like she wants to laugh.

Once we're done, Alenia asks, "Will the CloudsCorp ship be able to find us again?"

"With the engines off, there'll be too much interference," I say, shaking my head. "Plus, this wavelength reading here is getting smaller, which means they're going further away."

We all sigh in relief.

Jazz undoes the straps of her seat and floats back into the air.

"Let me see those directions," she demands, making grabby hand movements towards Alenia's holopad.

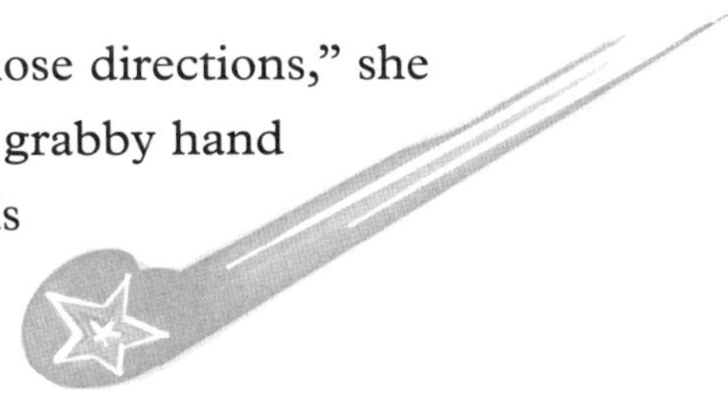

"We've got places to be! Inventions to present! Libraries to visit!"

I laugh. Jazz is right. We've got work to do if we're going to get home!

Chapter 10

Eventually, Jazz flies us out of the asteroid field, then a little further to make sure we're not being followed again. Then, once we're sure it's safe, she stops the ship briefly to let the solar panels charge up more before we keep flying.

It might take a little while to finish, so we all drift apart to do our own things.

I go to my room for a bit. After all that excitement, I need a chance to be alone again and just breathe.

Eventually though, the silence gets bad, and I start thinking too much about the stuff I'm trying to *not* think about. Like what if we can't find our way home? What if we stay lost *forever*?

I wanted to prove a galaxy existed, not get sucked into it and never see my mums again!

As those thoughts weigh down on me, I shove my way out of the bedroom and towards the holotable instead, looking for a distraction.

Luckily, the Apprentice 3's computers have all the basic Starfinder databases. I start on my tablet, pulling up data from my favourite old Earth spacecraft: the James Webb. It was a famous telescope that took all kinds of amazing pictures when humans started exploring the stars with spacecraft.

I grab a few good pictures from it and swipe them over to the holotable. Then I flip to the spacecraft data set.

Soon, I'm lost in pictures and charts, my favourite place to be.

"What's that?" asks Alenia, as I work.

"I'm making a gift," I explain, pausing as I decide between a picture from James Webb or a chart showing some radar readings from a satellite.

I go with the picture but swipe the radar readings back onto my holopad to save for later. "For my mum. I'm making her a scrapbook of pictures and data."

Alenia floats over to watch. I arrange three pictures on the holotable, the images floating just a little above it. Then I add a chart next to them.

"The data is all from Earth or near it. Earth's the planet Mum and I were born on," I explain, since Alenia seems interested. "For this, I started with a

picture of a painting from an ancient astronomer who studied the sky before humans even went to space. Then I got a picture from Hubble, which was a really cool old space telescope back in ancient times, and then I found a picture of the same spot from James Webb, another cool old space telescope. Then I'll try to find some charts showing radar data and stuff from the first Earth starship, then radar data AND pictures from the Starfinder spacecraft that first came to Earth 300 years ago."

"So, it's like a timeline using pictures and data?"

"Yeah!" I gesture to the stuff I've finished arranging. I've got a really cool page ready now showing off the Crab Nebula, an area of space where a star once went supernova and basically exploded. All I need is one final picture, and it'll be perfect.

"That's incredible!" Jazz chimes in. "Though I don't understand how you can stare at all those charts for so long."

She's floating up by the ceiling, flipping through a book of Mexican legends and folktales.

I squint at it. Yup, that's definitely a different book from the one she was reading earlier. Where are those even coming from? How did she fit so many books in her backpack?

"Data just makes sense to me," I say. "It's calming."

Jazz scrunches up her nose. "Yep. I do not understand."

"But reading sensor data is part of being a Starfinder," I argue. "We learn about it in every class."

"Yeah, but so is learning different stories and how to work with people." Jazz looks longingly up at the constellations painted across the ceiling. "I've never really liked the science stuff. I learn it as best as I can, but honestly, I want to be a diplomat."

"Like my mama?"

"Yeah! I want to visit different planets and learn about their stories and their history and stuff, and then help get people from those planets to become Starfinders too. I'll learn so many stories to take back home to my family. It'll make my *abuelo*, my grandfather, super proud. He's a storyteller and knows legends and folktales from all over Earth. I want to be just like him, except I'll learn stories from all across the universe!"

Suddenly, I feel embarrassed.

Here I am, judging Jazz this entire time because I don't understand her. Except, did I really even know Jazz?

I had no clue she could fly so well! Or that she could talk to people so well. Just look at how she helped make Alenia feel more comfortable earlier. And I didn't realise she's *also* trying to make somebody in her family proud.

Maybe Jazz isn't as different from me as I thought.

"You'll be a good Starfinder," I say. "I don't always understand how you can like stories or daydreaming so much, but that doesn't make what you do any less important."

I just wish I'd realised that sooner. I was so *mean.*

"I don't really understand you either,"

admits Jazz, with a grin. "I don't get why you like all the science stuff so much when people are way more important, but … You're also really good at what you do."

Alenia giggles. "It sounds like you both have talents your Starfinders need, which means that together you have everything covered."

I'd never thought about it like that before.

Maybe working with Jazz isn't a bad thing. Maybe it's the best thing that could happen, since Jazz can do the stuff I'm bad at and I can do the stuff Jazz doesn't care about.

Maybe we make better Starfinders together than we could ever be on our own.

Chapter 11

I'm feeling pretty good about things after talking to Jazz and Alenia. We've got a plan. We're on our way to the Planet of Many Sunsets. There's been no sign of the CloudsCorp ship since we ditched it earlier.

Things are looking up.

Then it happens. Just as the planet comes into view – still a tiny speck far in the distance – the Apprentice 3 makes a strange groaning sound.

Something *clicks*.

Something *THUNKS*.

Then our spacecraft jolts forward, shudders,

and the engines cut out. Creaking noises come from the engines.

They're not supposed to sound like that.

"Oh no." Jazz flips through the info screens. "Our engines aren't doing so well. I think they must've been damaged in the chase."

The engines start back up, jolting us forward again.

"Can we still reach the Planet of Many Sunsets?" asks Alenia.

"Yes … but I'm not sure if the engines will be good enough to help the ship land."

"What do you mean?" asks Alenia.

"Our spacecraft will keep flying forward until we get to the planet, since there's no gravity or anything to slow it down right now," I explain, remembering Newton's laws of motion. "So, we don't need the engines to get there now that we're already moving that way. Except – "

Alenia's face falls. "We need them to create

a counter force that can slow us down when we try to land."

"Yup."

I wince, looking around the little spacecraft. There are some tools in one of the metal cabinets for little fixes inside, but there's no way to actually reach the engines, and probably not the right tools to fix them anyway. The Apprentice 3 didn't need that, not when it wasn't made to go so far away from the starship.

"Aim for the planet's moon," Alenia says. "They've got special docking bays that have buffers to slow ships that are flying in too fast."

"I think the engines will last long enough to land there," Jazz says. "Let's try it."

Alenia bites her lip. "Then we can take a spacebus the rest of the way."

It takes almost the entire day to make it to the moon. Jazz doesn't want to risk going faster and breaking the engines even more. By the time we're there, our spacecraft is making all kinds of scary grinding and creaking sounds.

"Come on, Gerda, you can do it," whispers Jazz, as she pilots the ship towards the rocky grey surface of the moon. A massive planet – the gas giant – fills the sky beyond it.

"Gerda?"

"Yeah! It's a character from an old Earth fairy tale called *The Snow Queen*." Jazz smiles fondly. "Gerda has to save her friend, and never gives up, so I thought the name fitted."

"Yeah, it does," I had to admit.

We sit in silence after that and watch as we get closer to the gas giant. Swirling blue and tan clouds cover the surface, twisting alongside smatterings of milky white. It fills our entire viewscreen, the planet so big that it looks really close, even though I know it's still super far away.

Jazz aims for the small moon in front of it.

"Woah," I gasp, as we fly closer. This moon is *nothing* like the small, rocky moon that orbits Earth,

or any moon I've seen before. This moon is vibrant green, with plants *everywhere* and … "Are those floating cities?"

My eyes feel as wide as saucers.

Alenia laughs. "Yes! The air and plants on this moon are toxic to most people, so the cities float above the ground, protected by the bubbles."

Sure enough, there are great big bubbles around each floating city.

"This is so cool!" says Jazz, as she steers us towards one.

Our ship shudders and shakes as we land – the buffers ensure the ship doesn't crash in the small docking bay, but I'm pretty sure I hear something crack and splinter.

Still, Jazz lands us safely.

"I'm sorry, Gerda," she whispers to the spacecraft when we step outside, pressing a hand to the cold metal.

"I'll fix her for you," promises Alenia. "Once

we're done, we'll come back, and I'll fix her."

Then we're off, Alenia leading us past signs in a language I can't read, and towards the spacebus port.

The city is like nothing I've ever seen before. There's just enough gravity to keep us on the ground, but not nearly as much as on Earth, so we end up walking in kind of a hop-shuffle. Everything has a greenish colour from the light filtering in through the bubble, and there are people *everywhere*.

Jazz and I stare around with wide eyes.

People haggle about prices in front of brightly coloured food and knick-knack stalls. Sleek silver spacecraft fly in and out of the bubble overhead. The ground itself is made of some kind of sheer plastic material which lets us look all the way to the ground far below.

It's incredible.

At least, until Alenia comes to a sudden stop.

"That's a problem," she says, jutting her chin

out towards where a couple of people stand at the spacebus entrance. I think they're law enforcement, until I look closer and see the CloudsCorp logo on their clothing.

We all exchange a look.

They must be watching every spaceport and anywhere they think we might land. How are we supposed to get past them?

"We could disguise ourselves," suggests Jazz. She points over to a stall selling vests and hats and all

kinds of clothing.

"That won't work," grumbles Alenia. "Look. They're checking everyone closely. They'll recognise me faster than an imploding sun."

Sure enough, whenever somebody walks past, the CloudsCorp people hold up bulky holopad-like tablets. One shifts just enough that I can see the screen. There's a picture of Alenia on it.

"Ugh. But the spacebus leaves soon," groans Jazz. "We can't miss it!"

I frown, a million thoughts turning in my head. A disguise won't be enough on its own, not when Alenia also has her blueprints sticking out of her bag and is travelling with us. CloudsCorp may not have seen us inside our spacecraft, but they know that Alenia has help, and they must have noticed how different our spacecraft looks from anything in this solar system.

If they spot two people who also dress totally differently from anyone here, they'll pay more attention to our group. So, we can't just walk in, and a disguise might not be enough either. We need something else … We need …

"I know!" I spin around, looking for something that can help. Nearby, a woman is selling some sort of fizzy drink in shiny bottles. Perfect! "I have a plan. I can explain it, but it might take a bit of time."

Jazz fidgets with her sound dampeners, biting her lip like she's thinking. Then she shrugs. "I trust you, and we don't have much time left, so let's try it. You can explain later, if you want."

"Right. OK. So first I need you to – " I bite on my necklace and flap my other hand a little, trying to figure out exactly how to say it. "I need you to get some disguises for us, just like you were thinking."

Jazz and Alenia head for the clothing seller and I hurry over to the vendor with the bottles. I don't have money from this solar system to buy one with, but that's OK. Starfinders visit a lot of planets we've never been to before, so we're ready for that.

While I don't have any money, I do have some pretty star-shaped gemstones that the vendor is happy to trade a bottle of drink for.

Soon, I'm hurrying over to where Jazz and Alenia now have an armful of clothing. We all duck into a small alleyway and pull the clothing over our current stuff.

When we're done, Alenia's hair is hidden under a hat, her eyes are hidden by a fancy pair of glasses, and she's even swapped her vest for a jacket. Meanwhile, Jazz and I have hidden our Starfinder outfits underneath a mishmash of loose shirts and vests and even bulky cargo trousers like Alenia's.

I take the bottle and empty it out.

"Mama always likes to do science experiments with me," I explain, peering around the corner to watch the CloudsCorp people. "One of my favourite experiments was one she taught me when she was getting to know me, before she married Mum. She'd use glass bottles to show me how light changes when it's reflected through stuff, like how some satellites use reflected light to detect stuff we can't actually see."

I angle the bottle, so it catches the sunlight

from above. The light shines against the bottle and I'm able to create a small beam of light further down the street.

"Sometimes, we'd just use the bottles to make spots of light dance around instead; that was fun too."

"How will this help us?" Alenia asks, her brow furrowed in confusion.

"I'm going to angle the bottle, so the light reflects right across one of their screens. That should distract them a little. While they're distracted, you and Jazz hurry past. Then I'll follow afterwards."

"That's brilliant!" exclaims Jazz.

She and Alenia duck back into the street and start slowly walking towards the spacebus entrance. Once they get close, I tilt the bottle so it reflects light right across one of the CloudsCorp people's holopads. I hear grumbling as he tries to move his tablet out of the light, but I move the bottle again.

And again. And again.

He throws his hands in the air and goes to show

his colleague, loudly complaining that something's wrong with his holopad.

Jazz and Alenia use that moment to hurry past.

Then they are through, marching right over to the spacebus and onto it without any of the CloudsCorp people realising! It worked!

After a minute, I set down the bottle and hurry to follow them.

"That was amazing!" Alenia laughs, as the spacebus takes off. "They won't be able to stop me from presenting to the council now!"

Chapter 12

Everything moves in a blur after that.

Our spacebus lands on the gas giant. There's a big silvery building where we're able to rent masks and protective suits; the hydrogen air is toxic for anyone who breathes oxygen. Then we swim through the air over to the council building where Alenia shows an appointment card to the front desk in the building's lobby.

"Good luck!" I say, once she's ushered to a nearby door. She's practically hugging her blueprints as she goes.

"You've got this!" adds Jazz.

Alenia smiles, then disappears through the door.

There's not much else we can do, so Jazz and I wait and chat about what we'll do once we get home. Then finally …

"They loved it!" Alenia practically flies out of the door, laughing and smiling. "They loved it so much that they're sending the blueprints to all the best engineers around the solar system right now! Plus, they said I could get an apprenticeship to learn more alongside any engineer I want!"

"But you're already so good at engineering," laughs Jazz.

"Yes, but I want to learn more!" She flies to a stop in front of us, one hand held behind her back. "First though – "

With a big flourish, Alenia reveals three fancy silver rectangles, each with a picture of a book on the front.

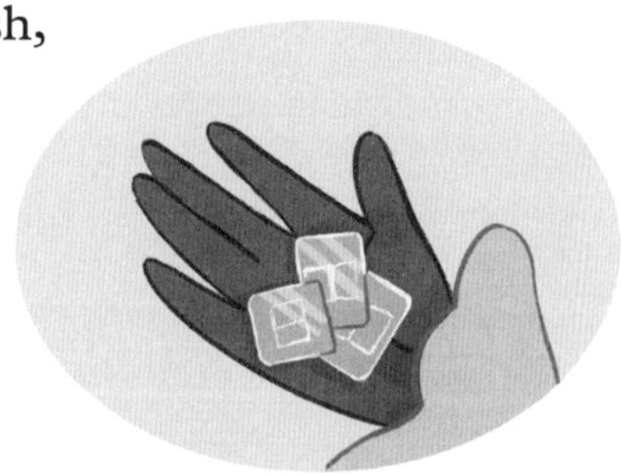

Library cards!

The Sunset Library is *amazing*.

We swim through the air to it from the council building, oohing and aahing over how massive it is. It's made of some sort of shiny silvery-gold metal and sits on a platform as long as three city blocks back on Earth.

We swipe our library cards at the door, and we're in!

Inside is just as amazing.

The space is full of books, all in clear sealed containers so they don't float away. Rows and rows of books, stretching out as far as we can see. There are also tables all around, and after a minute, I realise they're this solar system's version of holotables.

After I ask for directions to the star charts, we find a back corner of the library that has me opening and closing my mouth like a fish.

"Close your mouth and let's go and read," orders Alenia.

"Come on!" says Jazz.

They both swim towards the Star Chart corner, a section of the library with floor to ceiling star charts.

I spend the next hour taking pictures of as many star charts as I can with my holopad, then downloading even more from the library's digital database.

"Please let this work," I whisper, as I load them into the Star Map Collection.

Jazz and Alenia are looking over my shoulder at

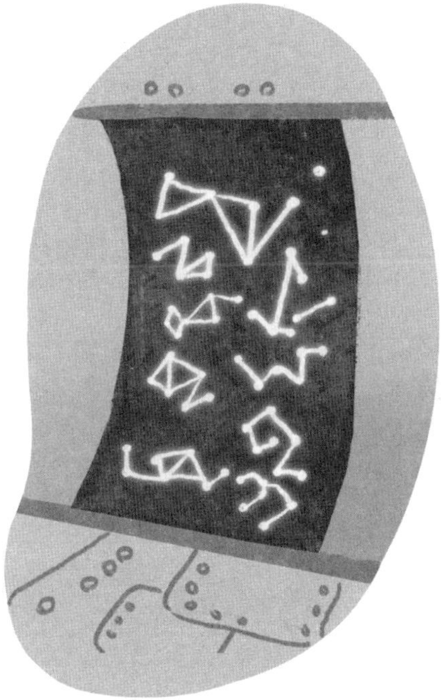

the holopad, while I adjust the settings in the app, then press **run**.

Images flash across my holopad. Map after map after map. Then …

Location Found

It worked! We have a way home!

Chapter 13

We spend another day at the library, even though we know how to get home.

Jazz desperately wants to read some of the books, Alenia ends up almost drooling over some engineering blueprints, and I can't resist reading about the sensors used by spacecraft in this solar system.

"Wait, you use anomalies as warp points?" I ask at one point, looking up from the journal of a famous space explorer.

"Yes! We have, ever since somebody discovered the technology 70 years ago. It's the most common way to travel around here now," says Alenia. "Don't you?"

Jazz and I both shake our heads.

"We didn't know what the anomaly was," Jazz admits.

"The people in our galaxies haven't figured out warp technology," I add, "but we have engineers that are trying to."

"Oh, we should fix that." Alenia turns back to the blueprint she was copying. "I'll add warp tech to your spacecraft. Then you can use any anomaly to jump to anywhere you want super-fast. Maybe I should come back to your galaxy with you."

"What about apprenticing as an engineer?" asks Jazz.

"I still want to do that," says Alenia. "But I can't decide who to work with. While I think about it, I'll come and meet your people instead."

With good news like that, there's no way I can focus on reading anymore.

The next day, we leave the library and take the spacebus back to the moon with the floating cities.

"I'm going to make your spaceship so much faster," Alenia says. She has a wrench in one hand and a wild look in her eyes. "Add warp technology, upgrade the engines … Oh, I can improve your water recycling system and air filters too!"

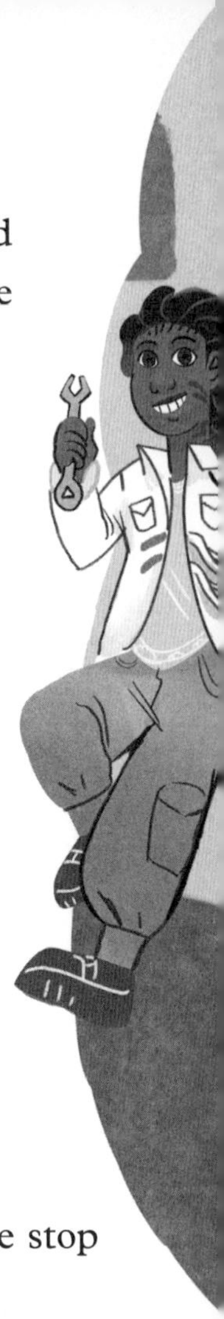

Jazz and I don't bother to point out that we just need the ship fixed.

Instead, we spend the day roaming around and shopping at the market stalls, buying everything we can to take home.

"I never told you why I wanted to do wavelength readings," I say to Jazz, when we stop at a stall selling candyfloss-like treats.

"Huh?"

"During the test. You wanted to take pictures, but I insisted on wavelength readings."

"Oh, yeah. What was that about?"

I explain everything to Jazz, all about how I had uncovered data that hinted at an unknown galaxy. How badly I wanted to make my mothers proud of me, and to live up to their reputation as amazing Starfinders. How Varl and I were going to try and get proof of the galaxy during the test, and how I'm pretty sure we're now in the very place I wanted to find.

"I think this solar system is right on the edge of that galaxy," I finish.

"Wow!" gasps Jazz. "That's amazing."

"Yeah! But, I should have told you sooner. We're a team, and we could have worked together during the test if I wasn't so stubborn. Maybe we wouldn't have got lost in the first place."

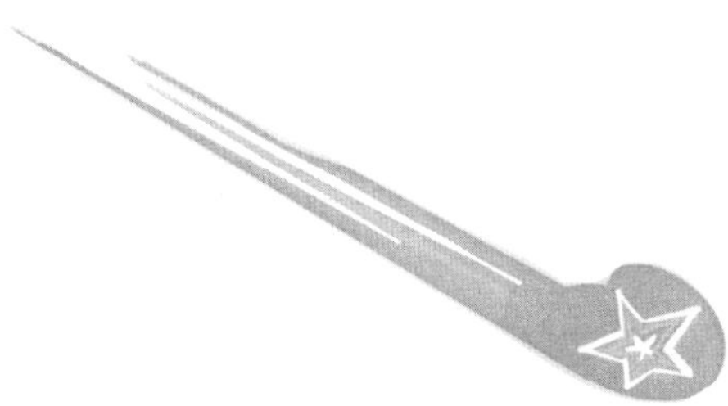

Jazz spins towards me and grins. "That's OK! We got to meet Alenia because of it! Plus, this has been super fun. We'll probably be in so much trouble when we get home though."

"Yeah – " I hunch my shoulders.

"Cheer up!" laughs Jazz. "We'll definitely be in trouble, but we get to introduce the Starfinders to Alenia and tell them about this place. Our families and friends are going to be so amazed!"

That does help me feel better.

Mum and Mama will be furious, because they're probably so scared right now wondering what happened to me. But knowing my mothers, they'll also be really proud of how Jazz and I handled everything after we got stuck here.

Whatever else happens, the future's going to be really exciting.

"Come on," I say, grinning. "Alenia's got to be done upgrading the ship by now."

"I bet Gerda doesn't even look the same after all those upgrades!" laughs Jazz.

Then we're off, heading back to the docking port and our friend.

Soon, we'll be home. I can't wait to tell Varl, Lizel and my mothers all about the adventure we had. We'll help write peace treaties and map so many stars and learn from an entire new galaxy full of brilliant

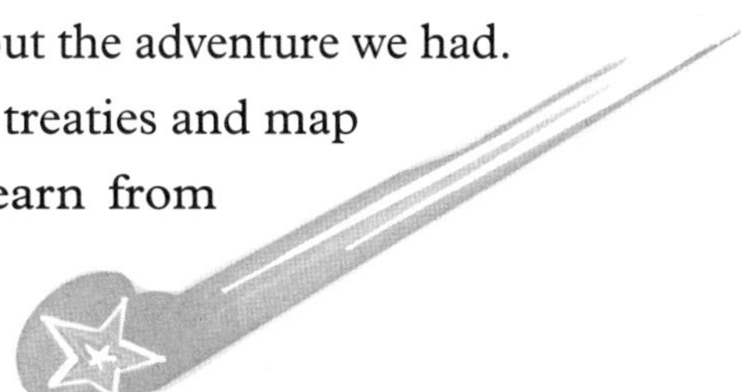

people like Alenia. Soon, we'll have a whole future to dive into, two Starfinders and an engineer working as a team.

I can't wait to get started!

Book talk questions

Would you like to be a Starfinder?

How does Rowan's relationship with Jazz evolve over the course of their adventure?

Why do you think it's important that everyone is different?

What are the most memorable moments for Rowan and Jazz as they travel through space?

How do Rowan and Jazz react to the strange and unfamiliar worlds they visit?

What are the challenges of being trapped in a galaxy far from home?

How does the book explore the themes of friendship and personal growth?

What kind of characters do Rowan and Jazz meet on their journey, and how do they help the story?

What does Rowan learn about leadership and responsibility?

How does the story balance action and emotional moments in space exploration?

Ask the author

Which character do you most identify with in the book?

Rowan AND Jazz! I absolutely adore space, just like Rowan, but I also love stories like Jazz does. I daydream all the time too, just like Jazz.

Michelle Mohrweis

What do you enjoy about writing?

I love the possibilities that writing creates. I can write anything, can use my stories to dream of what might someday be possible! I can explore emotions and challenges you and I deal with every day, but in new places and while on amazing adventures.

What inspired you to write a story about space exploration and starfinders?

One of my favourite things is to watch videos of Earth passing underneath the International Space Station, a science lab that's in space right now! I got the idea for this story when I was thinking about how amazing it would be to see not just Earth from space, but other planets too someday.

Do you have a favourite place to write?

I do! I really like to write outside, on a little patio in my backyard. I often walk in circles and write my stories using speech to text software while I walk!

What do you want readers to take away from Rowan's and Jazz's journey?

Everyone matters and everyone has their own strengths, just like Rowan, Alenia and Jazz.

What do you like to do for fun?

My favourite hobbies include watching videos from the space station, reading and 3D printing!

How did you come up with the concept of a "Starfinder" and what it means?

People have been looking to the stars throughout human history. Early astronomers learnt so much about our universe from the stars, sailors used the stars to navigate, and so many cultures have stories about the constellations that stars make. I wanted to write a future where we are still always looking for and learning from new stars and the planets around them. From there, "Starfinder" just made sense as the name of these future people.

Collins
BIG CAT

Published by Collins
An imprint of HarperCollins*Publishers*

The News Building
1 London Bridge Street
London SE1 9GF
UK

Macken House
39/40 Mayor Street Upper
Dublin 1
D01 C9W8
Ireland

10 9 8 7 6 5 4 3 2 1

ISBN 978-0-00-874480-9

British Library Cataloguing-in-Publication Data
A catalogue record for this publication is available from the British Library.

Author: Michelle Mohrweis
Illustrator: Fran Cesarano (Astound)
Publisher: Laura White
Commissioning editor: Holly Woolnough
Development editor: Zoë Clarke
Product manager: Holly Woolnough
Content editor: Selin Akca
Copyeditor: Sally Byford
Proofreader: Catherine Dakin
Reviewer: Lisa Davis
Sensitivity reader: Sophie Williamson
Cover designer: Sarah Finan
Internal design: 2Hoots Publishing Services Ltd
Typesetter: Jouve India Ltd
Production controller: Katharine Willard

Collins would like to thank the teachers and children at Grange Primary School, Southwark, for being part of the development of Big Cat Read On.

Printed in the UK

FSC www.fsc.org
MIX
Paper | Supporting responsible forestry
FSC™ C007454

This book contains FSC™ certified paper and other controlled sources to ensure responsible forest management.

For more information visit: www.harpercollins.co.uk/green

Made with responsibly sourced paper and vegetable ink

Scan to see how we are reducing our environmental impact.